HUNTED
HIGHGATE PREPARATORY ACADEMY PREQUEL

ROSA LEE

Copyright © 2024 by Rosa Lee

All rights reserved.

No part of this book may be reproduced in any form or by any electronic or mechanical means, including information storage and retrieval systems, without written permission from the author, except for the use of brief quotations in a book review.

Cover design provided by Jodilock Designs

BLURB

Pregnant.

Funny how one small word can change the course of your life so completely that it becomes unrecognisable.

In order to protect the life growing inside me, I must change who I am, escaping from the rich yet depraved mountains of Colorado to the hidden exclusivity of London.

Dancing becomes my freedom, giving me everything that I've missed from my privileged life so far. Friends, safety and a fresh start.

But, you can't outrun your past forever.

And it's only a matter of time before mine catches up with me...

*** For 18+ Hunted is a Highgate Preparatory Academy Prequel and is told from the POV of Laura Darling, Lilly's mother. It contains mention and scenes of explicit sexual nature, violence and domestic abuse. If you find any of these things triggering probably best to leave now.

Hunted Playlist

I love books with playlists and I listen to my compiled playlist as I'm writing. I've even based some scenes solely around one track, let me know if you guess which ones! And you'll see a lot of the music mentioned in the book itself.

Listen to the full playlist on Spotify <u>HERE</u>

FOREWORD

Dear Reader,

Firstly, thank you so much for taking a chance on me and reading *Hunted*. I hope you enjoy it!

Also, as you may already know that I am British and so *Hunted* is written in a mix of British and American English. This has been done on purpose, to reflect the different characters and their cultures, so some words will be spelled differently throughout depending on who's speaking or thinking! If you see some unfamiliar words, know that they are there intentionally and I hope you enjoy discovering new phrases!

As mentioned in the blurb, *Hunted* is a dark romance. There are many subjects explored that some readers may find disturbing.

For a full list of triggers please visit www.rosaleeauthor.com/trigger-warnings

Also a small word of caution. My books have a lot of BDSM vibes in them, and if they inspire you to dive into that kinky world, please do your research and educate yourself before trying out anything new for the first time. Take care my little smut bunnies!

CHAPTER ONE

Pregnant.
 I sit on the toilet, the test shaking in my hand, making that one word jump and dance around, as if taunting me. A gasping sob falls from my lips, my other hand coming up quickly to cover the sound.

Funny how one small word can change the course of your life so completely that it becomes unrecognisable.

Shit. I can't have a child with him. I think, panic flaring in my chest as images of flying fists flash across my mind.

A bang on the door makes me jump, dropping the stick which goes skittering across the expensive black marble tiled flooring.

"Coming!" I shout, standing and pulling my knickers back up my legs, letting my midnight blue silk evening gown fall to the floor. My hand traces over my stomach, as if I can feel the life growing inside of me, which of course is impossible as according to the test, I'm only a few weeks along.

"Violet," a deep voice sounds on the other side of the door, and I shudder at the dark tone. "You'll make us late."

"Just washing up, Ace," I call out, turning the tap on, then picking up the test and frantically looking around for somewhere to hide it. He can't see it, not until I've decided what I'm going to do. Spotting the under sink cupboard, I quickly stash it behind all of the cleaning products.

I'll have to come back for it later.

After washing my hands, I take a final look in the mirror. My dress has a high neck and back, and you can only just see a faint purple mark peeking out from under the collar. The rest of the dress hugs my figure, with rhinestones covering down to my hips and glittering like stars in the night sky. They lessen as the skirts flare out around my feet in a swishing mermaid tail.

I take a deep breath to steady myself, wincing as my bruised ribs twinge.

Just get through this evening, then think about what to do next.

I plaster a smile on my face, grabbing my matching beaded purse off the counter, and open the door to find Ace, my fiancé, standing in a full black tuxedo and looking devilishly handsome. His hair is thick and a dark chocolate brown slicked back from his arresting face. His jaw is sharp, his nose straight like a Roman emperor's, and there's a neat, dark beard covering his jawline.

It's a beautiful face, but a hard one, and right now, his thick brows are pinched over his dark brown eyes. Had I looked closer when I first met him, I might have noticed the deadness lurking just beneath the surface of those shadowy orbs. Not that it would have made much of a difference, I suppose. This is an arranged match, one both our parents decided when we were in the cradle. Contracts signed and sealed before our first birthday.

Those sable eyes take me in; starting at my lightly made up face, moving down my silk-clad body, assessing my appearance for any flaw, and leaving unpleasant tingles in their wake. Finding none, he nods and holds out one arm for me to take. I rush in my heels to do so, knowing that any infraction will be paid for later behind closed doors.

"I don't like to be kept waiting, Violet." He admonishes as we leave the house, walking towards the waiting black SUV, and Tom, our driver. "You know they'll try and steal any advantage they can. Bunch of ignorant jackals." His lip curls, tone scathing, and I wonder, not for the first time, why he went into business with the others if he finds them so distasteful. We all went to high school together, and they always seemed pretty tight knit.

Ace and I went to school here in Colorado, and Highgate Preparatory Academy is one of the best in the world, especially for meeting future business associates and leaders. The teaching is second to none, but it's the connections and networking with the top one-percenters that is the real draw. It surprised me when my English parents suggested it, but then again, since Ace is American and was coming here, it only made sense for me to come as well given our betrothal.

Once we'd graduated, I wanted to go on and study something artistic, history of art in New York perhaps, but Ace had other plans so we ended up at Yale School of Management earning our MBAs there. I should have known then what sort of man he was, but I was too meek, too desperate for affection, after a lack of any sort from my stiff and emotionally distant parents.

We graduated this summer and moved into a large mansion about twenty minutes from Brompton Lakes, back near Highgate Prep. It's got more rooms than we need and is secluded in the woods; nice and private just as Ace likes. No nosy neighbours to interfere with his pleasures.

Tonight, we're on our way to the official opening gala of Black Knight Corporation, the multifaceted company that Ace has set up with Julian Vanderbilt, Rafe Griffiths, Stephen Matthews, and Chad Thorn. All rich, entitled brats with pretty faces that hide their twisted and depraved personalities.

The SUV stops, snapping me out of my musings, and Tom gets out and comes to open Ace's door.

He turns to me, dark eyes almost black and boring into my very soul. "Best behaviour, Violet. Don't show me up tonight." He doesn't wait for an answer, just steps out of the vehicle, and then leans back to hold a hand out like the perfect gentleman.

A plan starts to formulate in my mind as I sit through dinner followed by rounds of self-congratulatory speeches. Over the past couple of years, I've perfected the art of smiling like I'm engaged whilst my mind wanders. No one really cares, women are just arm candy to these fat cats and corrupt leaders.

I open my purse, looking around to make sure that no eyes are on me. As usual, they're too focused on themselves to notice as I slip some powder into Ace's champagne flute whilst he's in the bathroom. I've got about fifteen to twenty minutes before the effects kick in, so I've made sure we're getting towards the end of the evening.

It's Rohypnol, and until recently, he was using it on me without my knowledge. Some mornings I'd wake up with new bruises and an ache between my thighs, yet have no clue how they got there until I saw him drugging my drink a few months back.

We were at a function, not dissimilar to this one, with rich men trying to line their pockets and Ace schmoozing his way around. I'd popped to the bathroom, returning sooner than he clearly expected, and saw him slip something into my glass. I managed to ditch the drink when he wasn't looking, only to face his puzzled anger later on in the evening once we'd arrived back at the house.

It didn't take much to put two and two together, and realise what he'd been up to and why I had gaps in my memories.

A few days later, when he was away for a business meeting, aka a prostitute orgy, I stole his stash. Black Knight Corp has a pharmaceutical arm, run by Rafe Griffiths, which explains how Ace managed to get a hold of the drug in the first place. Bunch of bloody criminals hiding behind lily white family reputations, bought of course. I knew I couldn't just take the drug without risking his notice. I'd need to replace it with something, so I replaced it with a placebo, that way I was at least aware of what was happening.

I've used the Rohypnol on him a few times; he gets especially aggressive after these sorts of events, so I pretended he just drank a lot and passed out. It seems to have worked so far, even with his control freak tendencies.

Ace gets up after he finishes his glass, indicating it's time to head back to the house. He stumbles as we walk through the tables, his already tight grip on my arm tightening further, and I know I'll have more bruises tomorrow.

"Must have drunk more than I thought," he mumbles as we step into the cool fall air. Tom is already waiting and helps me get Ace into the SUV, his hand brushing mine as he pulls away, sending pleasurable shivers down my arm.

"Home?" he asks me quietly. His blue eyes boring into mine then flicking to Ace.

"Yes please, Tom," I whisper back. His gaze flits to my neck, likely noticing the bruises peeking out of my collar. His whole body hardens, and his chiselled jaw clenches as he starts to reach out towards me.

"Don't," I plead, which stops him in his tracks. A look of frustration comes over his face, then he huffs out a breath, looking ahead as I climb in next to Ace, Tom shutting the door behind me.

The journey is short, Ace unconscious the whole time. He should be out for several hours which gives me plenty of time to put my plan into action.

We pull up outside of the house, and I look up, seeing Tom's blue gaze in the rearview mirror, his dark blond hair pushed off his forehead. A sudden image of me running my hands through its softness, and feeling his stubbled jaw under my lips, flashes through my mind. My breath hitches at the memory.

"Can you help me with him please, Tom?" I ask, voice quiet. I don't dare utter my other request until Ace is tucked up into bed.

"Of course," he practically growls, getting out of the car and opening Ace's door.

Tom grabs him, cracking Ace's head on the frame as he pulls him out of the car. Hoisting Ace up over his shoulder, he walks up the path as I follow behind, stepping up to open the door. Tom carries him up the stairs, going to Ace's bedroom, and throws him onto the bed before turning to face me.

I put a finger to his lips before he can utter a word, shaking my head. He indicates the door, and I pull my hand back, turning around and leaving the room. I walk to my bedroom, opening the door, and stepping inside. Tom is quick on my heels, leaving the door slightly ajar as he, too, steps inside.

"Let me see," he asks, voice firm and eyes pained.

I reach behind me and undo the collar, letting the dress slink down to the floor in a whisper of jewels. Tom lets out a hiss as he catalogues all the new bruises littering my torso. Before now, I've tried to keep the worst of the bruising from him, it's not like we get a lot of time together so it hasn't been too difficult to do.

"I'm going to fucking kill him," he fumes, making a move to step back through the door. He could take him too, they are evenly matched in stature and muscle. But Tom lacks Ace's cruelty, and that would be his downfall if they ever came to blows.

"No!" I rush over, gripping his muscular bicep tightly to stop him. "Tom, please, I need your help," I beg quietly. That pulls him up short, but I can see his chest heaving, and he's vibrating with anger. "I need to leave tonight, and I need you to help me."

"Why now?" he asks. It's a fair question, he's pleaded with me to leave Ace before, and I've always been too scared, so I refused. But it's not just me anymore. I take his hand and place it over my stomach. His eyes widen in the darkness, and I feel his warm hand flex as he lightly caresses me there.

"What do you need?" he murmurs, hand still splayed over my stomach protectively.

"You mentioned before that your new brother-in-law, Enzo, has connections and can get things in and out of the country without a trace?" I question a brief flicker of hope flaring to life inside of me.

He nods, understanding straight away what I'm asking.

"And I need a new identity that no one knows." He nods again, his brows pinching a little.

"He can do that, I think," he replies, his voice deep and soothing to me as it always is. My breath whooshes out of me as relief floods through my body, leaving my knees weak.

"Right," I say shakily. "I need to change and grab a few things."

I head towards my closet, stopping in the doorway. I have no idea what to take with me. As I dither, wasting precious seconds, I feel his warmth at my back. I want to lean into the comfort, but I manage to hold back, remaining upright. "I don't know what to take," I confess in a whisper, a lump in my throat.

"Comfortable clothes to travel in, things you can easily sell," Tom says decisively, stepping into the closet and reaching for a duffel bag on a shelf. It spurs me into action, and I start grabbing underwear, jeans, and tops from various drawers and stuffing them into the bag. When it's full, I turn to leave but stop as his warm hand lands on my bare waist.

"You might want to get dressed, Vi." Tom chuckles from behind me, his breath tickling the back of my neck.

"Oh, yes," I mumble, my cheeks flaming. I step past him and quickly dress in some dark jeans, a long-sleeved top, a cashmere sweater, and my comfy leather boots. Grabbing my warm winter coat, I turn back, smiling at him.

"Ready," I announce, voice still low. I know that Ace is out for the next four to six hours, but I can't help feeling like he's going to wake up any minute.

We head out of the bedroom then down the stairs, and Tom starts to head towards the front door.

"I'll be there in a minute," I softly tell him as he looks back when he notices that I'm not following. He frowns but waits by the door as I make my way to Ace's office.

I step inside and head straight to the desk, fear of even being in here hastening my steps. Behind the desk is a safe, and I crouch down, the moonlight lighting the keypad just enough for me to see. I discovered the code one day when Ace made me stand behind the desk for twenty-four hours with no food or drink for accidentally shrinking one of his cashmere jumpers in the wash.

I still breathe out a sigh of relief when the door clicks open. It's not that full as far as safes go, and there's a reason as to why his family wants mine. I find the stack of papers that I need, bonds for the company that were purchased using an advance of my dowry. *Yes, I've got an honest to god dowry!*

The next thing I take is an ornate wooden jewellery box. It contains old heirloom pieces all belonging to my family and now me. It's mine by rights anyway, and I can maybe exchange the pieces for my passage.

Closing the safe, I stand up and head out of the room, hurrying to Tom who just looks at the items then takes them from me and puts them into my bag. He opens the door, letting in the refreshing night air, and I take a deep breath as I step through.

Freedom tastes like falling leaves and damp earth, and I can't stop the smile tugging at my lips as we drive away.

CHAPTER TWO

We arrive on the other side of town, the streets dark and empty as we drove. Pulling up outside a squat concrete building, I notice the windows are black, yet there's someone waiting for us in front of the plain wooden door as we step out of the car.

Tom gets my bag from the boot, then takes my hand and leads me up to what I now see is a man who is maybe ten years older than us, around mid-thirties. He's got swarthy Italian looks, black hair greased back, and deep brown eyes. Although unlike Ace's, there's a warmth and kindness in their depths.

Even though it's the middle of the night and autumn, he's wearing a black wife beater that shows off his arms that are covered in colourful, old school style tattoos. They're beautiful and a stark contrast to his all black outfit.

He smiles wide as we approach. "Brother, *fratello mio!*" he whispers jovially, his Italian accent strong. He opens his arms and embraces Tom, who doesn't let go of my hand, so it's slightly awkward. "*Che piacere...*Good to see you, although I wish it were under better circumstances...*purtroppo*."

He turns to me, his eyes softening with sympathy. "You must be Violet?" He asks me gently, and I nod, holding my free hand out to shake his.

He surprises me by grasping it and pulling forward, forcing Tom to finally let go with a growl, while kissing both of my cheeks continental style.

"Pleased to meet you, *molto piacere*." He grins, and he has such an aura of safety and warmth that I can't help but grin back. "I'm Enzo, Tom's brother by marriage. Although, I think he already told you that, *si? Forse?*" He asks, still grinning and not waiting for my answer. "Let's get you inside and see what's to be done...*prego.*"

He ushers us inside, Tom grabbing my hand once again, where I see a couple of others waiting around what looks and smells like a boxing gym. Tom's hand tightens around my grip, pulling me back slightly. I hear Enzo chuckle as he looks back at us.

"These are my cousins, and I'd trust them with my life, *cari veramente*," he tells Tom, who gives an imperceptible dip of his head, but still keeps a firm grip on my hand.

Enzo takes us to what I assume is his office and hands me a brown packet. I open it to find a British passport, Canada Air flight tickets, and other documents all with the name Laura Darling on them. My eyes prick with tears as I look up at him, gratitude washing through me.

"Thank you," I whisper, and his eyes go even softer.

"No problem, *cara mia*," he says gently back, smiling softly at me. "*Allora!* We have a shipment leaving tonight for Toronto, so you'll get there around ten tomorrow evening. I've booked you a flight to Dublin for six AM the day after, your tickets are in the pack. There will be someone to collect you from the airport and drive you across the border to Belfast, then you will take the ferry to Liverpool...*a posto*," he tells me, face serious.

I can't say anything, overwhelmed at his kindness. I didn't realise people like this existed. People who do things for others because it's the right thing to do.

"From there, *cara mia*, it's up to you to disappear." His brown eyes cloud a little with sadness, as he looks briefly to Tom whose jaw is clenched tightly.

My heart starts pounding in my chest, and my breath catches in my throat. In the rush to escape and the relief of finally starting my journey towards freedom, I didn't consider that I'd have to leave him behind. I suddenly feel lost at sea, as if my one security net has been severed. Tom is the only thing I've ever chosen for myself, and I suddenly realise that he's my safe haven, my rock, and now I have to let him go.

This is like no other pain I've ever known. All of Ace's beatings, humiliations, and sexual assaults can't even begin to compare to the crushing hurt inside my soul at the thought of leaving Tom behind.

It's not safe for him to come with me. Ace would know immediately, and Tom's family would suffer terribly. His sister Rosa would be a target, regardless of Enzo's connections. I shudder at the thought of what Ace will do in his rage. Who he might hurt...

Tears fill my eyes as I look up into Tom's blue ones. They're usually so light and full of laughter, but tonight they are swirling, like a sea raging with Poseidon's wrath.

"Tom..." my voice breaks on a sob, and all of a sudden, I'm in his arms and they're banded around me so tightly I can hardly breathe. I welcome the embrace, the twinge of my bruised ribs as I sob against his chest, leaving a wet patch on his shirt.

"It'll be okay, Vi," he murmurs in my ear, voice rough and broken, stroking my back. "I'll find you one day, I swear it." I can hear the finality in his voice, like his promise is carved in stone. He knows as well as I do that he can't come with me right now.

"You need to go, *cara mia*," I hear Enzo say softly.

I take a huge gulping breath, somehow finding the strength to let go even though my world is crumbling down around me. I look up once more into his beautiful blue eyes.

"I love you, Tom," I whisper, unable to stop my tears from falling.

"I love you, Violet," he whispers back, lowering his lips to mine and kissing me. It's a kiss full of heartbreak, longing, and shattered dreams. We both know that there may never be a time that is safe for us to be together.

Our kiss ends on a shuddering breath, then he lowers his arms, jaw working once more as he takes a step back. Then another. And another until he turns and walks away, out of the office. I hear his footsteps echo across the silent gym floor, then the main door opens and shuts. Then finally, the sound of a car driving away.

Another breath catches in my throat, and I close my eyes, gathering my pieces up off the floor before opening them again. I meet Enzo's kind brown gaze, giving him a watery smile.

"Prego, this way, *cara mia*," he indicates the doorway, and we walk out, his hand on my lower back.

He guides me towards another door at the back of the building, where his two cousins are waiting for us. He says something to them sternly in Italian, and they nod once before bowing their heads in respect.

Then he turns to me, placing both hands on my upper arms.

"*In bocca al lupo*. All the luck in the world, cara mia," he says warmly, but I don't miss the glint of sorrow in his eyes.

"How can I ever repay you, Enzo?" I ask, knowing that I can never fully pay him back. He's helped me in my first steps towards my freedom. A shudder of unease runs through my whole body when I think back to Ace, his prone form lying on the bed. *Please let the drug work. I only need a few hours.*

"No payment needed, *cara mia*," he assures me. "*Abbiamo tutti diritto di Essere liberi di volare come gli uccelli*." I look at him questioningly. "We all deserve to be free, to fly like birds."

As I clutch the packet in my hands to my chest, I remember the gaudy engagement ring that Ace gave me. It's obscene, and he took great pains to tell me of its value.

"Take this," I plead, taking the bauble off my finger and handing it to him. "It's worth over three million dollars, and I can't take it with me. I don't want to."

"*Cara...* " he starts, and I can see he wants to refuse so I cut him off.

"I insist. Give the money to Rosa." I hold it out to him, begging him with my eyes to take it.

He sighs, but eventually relents and pockets the jewellery.

"Just be careful where you get rid of it. He will recognise it." I tell him and he nods, with a slight roll of his eyes as if to assure me he's not a rookie in situations such as these.

I grin at him, then press up to my tiptoes and place a soft kiss onto his cheek. I notice his cheeks darken slightly in the moonlight as I pull away.

"*Buon viaggio*, safe journey, cara mia," he whispers, taking my hands in his warm grip and kissing both my cheeks.

"Thank you." I smile back, taking a deep breath of crisp autumn air.

Turning my back to him, I step up to the open door of the car that'll take me on the next step to freedom. I get in while one of Enzo's guys places my bag next to me before shutting the door quietly behind me.

A strange mix of desperate sadness, fear, and elation churn within me as we drive away. My hand goes to rest on my stomach, and I know that this is the right decision. That I would do so much more to keep the life blooming inside me safe.

CHAPTER THREE

I spend the next few days in a permanent state of anxious exhaustion. The route Enzo picked out isn't the quickest or easiest, but it's thorough and I'm fairly confident that Ace won't be able to track me down, even with his endless resources.

As a precaution, once I arrive in Liverpool, I head to a pawn shop near the docks and sell some of the jewellery for cash, then go to the nearest salon. I emerge a fiery redhead, instead of my usual brunette, a colour admittedly, I've always wanted to be.

I decide to take the coach to London. I grew up in Surrey, and we visited the London house a few times so I know it well enough to feel comfortable there. I also like the idea of getting lost in the big city; there's a comfort of being around so many people. I know that it might be risky, it's one of the places that Ace may look for me, but if I avoid any of my previous haunts, I should be able to blend in with the throng.

The journey from Liverpool takes six long hours. Luckily, I bought a phone before I boarded the coach, and downloaded Spotify so I could at least listen to music and podcasts. I arrive at Victoria Coach Station just before ten in the evening, weary but glad that I'm almost to my new home.

It's still pretty busy, even for this late at night, and lucky for me it's not raining, as it so often is in England. My next task is to find somewhere to stay for tonight. I spy an open café across the street that looks like a good place to work out how I'm going to do that and grab a drink.

The sound of a bell tinkles as I push open the door, and I'm immediately engulfed in the warm smell of coffee and bacon. There's an empty table in the corner of the room next to the window, so I head there and take a seat. The whole place has that quaint vintage vibe about it, with mismatched chairs and old china plates, cups, and saucers. What sounds like wartime songs are playing in the background, alongside the hiss of the coffeemaker.

There are a few patrons, travellers like myself for the most part, all nursing steaming cups, and despite the late hour, one or two even have plates of a full English breakfast in front of them. There's a group of stunning women in the back, laughing and talking loudly, dressed in glittering party dresses that sparkle under the lights. I must admit, it's nice to be surrounded by the familiar sound of English voices again after hearing the American twang for so long.

One of the women, a busty brunette with green eyes, catches my gaze and gives me a blinding smile. I tentatively return the gesture, then look quickly down at the menu. I can't help the flinch as a shadow falls across the table, but breathe a sigh of relief when I look up to see a middle-aged waitress in a flowery fifties-style dress smiling down at me.

"What'll it be, luv?" she asks, her accent pure East End.

"Earl Grey tea, please. And maybe some toast and jam?" I ask timidly.

"Sure thing, luv," she answers with another smile before turning and heading back towards the counter.

Taking my phone out, I'm relieved to see that I've got a 4G signal and start looking up cheap hotels for the night. I figure I'll stay in one tonight and start flat hunting tomorrow.

A shadow falls across the table again, and I look up with a smile, placing my phone down and expecting to see the waitress with my order. My smile freezes as I meet the bloodshot eyes of a skinny man, with dark greasy hair and a lecherous grin.

"Hello, beautiful," he coos, and a shudder of revulsion passes through me at the state of his blackened teeth.

"Please leave me alone," I reply firmly, although there's a tremor in my hands now.

"Aw, there's no need to be like that," he says, leaning down so I can smell his rancid breath. "I was just bein' friendly like. And it looks like you're all alone and need a friend, eh?"

"I'm fine, thank you," I retort dismissively, hoping that he will leave me be.

Suddenly, his hand shoots out and grabs my wrist, his grip tight and painful. I try to snatch my hand back, but his hold is like a vice.

"Let go," I order through gritted teeth, panic starting to claw its way through me.

"You best let her go, Kol." A husky female voice sounds, and I crane my neck to see the beautiful brunette behind him, hands on her voluptuous hips. "This isn't your patch, and you wouldn't want Grey getting wind of this now, would you?" One of her perfect brows is raised, and there's a smug look on her face, like she knows she's already won.

Kol's upper lip curls, holding my wrist for a second longer before letting go with a snarl. He turns around and storms out, letting the door slam behind him. The effect is ruined somewhat by the cheery tinkle of the bell, and I can't help a small chuckle escaping my lips.

"Thanks," I say gratefully, rubbing my wrist.

"No worries, gorgeous. Kol is a disgusting shit face pimp, and he was overstepping," she informs me, insinuating herself into the chair opposite mine. There's no other word for the movement, she's so graceful with a sensuality about her it would be impossible for her to move any other way. "I'm Lexi," she tells me, holding out a manicured hand for me to shake.

"V-Laura," I say, tripping over my new name. *Dammit!* "Laura Darling. Pleased to meet you." I let go of her hand, dropping mine onto my lap nervously.

"Pleased to meet you, Laura." She beams at me. "Would I be right in assuming that you're new to London?" she asks tentatively, ducking her head to catch my lowered gaze. I nod, my nerves making my heart race. "Do you have a place to stay tonight, Laura?" she asks gently, and there's something so honest about her that I want to trust her.

My gut tells me she's good people, but then my gut didn't warn me about Ace so it doesn't exactly have a great track record.

"No," I whisper quietly, and all she does is smiles kindly at me.

"Well, I have a spare bed that you're welcome to, although we're on our way to Grey's so it would need to be after that." She pauses as if in thought, then snaps her fingers. "Do you have a job yet, Laura?" she asks, and I can hear the excitement in her voice.

"No." I sound like a broken record.

"Grey is looking for a new waitress if you're interested?" She looks so hopeful, like she truly wants to help me.

"I-I've never done waitressing before..." I hesitate.

"Oh, that's not a problem." She laughs, the sound like cigar smoke caressing me. "Leave Grey to me."

"I-I'm not sure..." I reply, not wanting to look a gift horse in the mouth, but how can I trust someone I've only just met?

It's at that moment, the waitress comes back with my order.

"Babs will tell you I'm alright, won't you, Babs?" Lexi assures me, looking up at her.

Babs, chuckles. "Lexi's a good 'un, luv," she assures me. "She'll see you right as rain." Setting down my order, she pats my shoulder then heads off again.

I chew my lip, trying to decide if I dare take the risk. My eyes snap up to Lexi's, who looks so encouraging, I decide to throw caution to the wind.

"Okay," I manage before she claps her hands in glee and hollers to the others in the back.

"Ladies! This is Laura, and she'll be joining us tonight!" They all cheer, and their enthusiasm is infectious, causing my lips to split into a wide grin. A fissure of excitement runs through me.

"Finish your tea and toast, gorgeous," Lexi commands me jovially. "Then we'll take you to Grey's."

CHAPTER FOUR

We head out of the cafe, and there's a big black stretch limo with blue neon lights underneath it waiting for us out front. It's got a grey smoke design across the doors, which I assume is the logo for Grey's.

I hesitate slightly, but I've agreed to come this far and don't really have many other options so I figure what the hell.

There are five of us in total; myself and Lexi, plus Coco who's a stunning dark-skinned woman with deep chocolate eyes, an awesome afro, and legs for days. Then, there's Anastasia, a beautiful leggy blonde with captivating green eyes full of saucy mischief and high cheekbones that any model would envy. Finally, there's Domitille, or Dom as she told me in a seductive French accent. A stunning redhead, with a beautiful hourglass figure and a wicked sense of humour.

The inside of the limo is lit up with LED strip lighting, and *Sex on Fire* by Kings of Leon is blasting out of the speakers as we step in. The girls start singing along, laughing as Coco grabs a bottle of champagne from somewhere and starts pouring glasses. She indicates the bottle to me, and I'm about to nod when I remember my condition and shake my head instead.

She just shrugs and puts the bottle away. I catch Lexi's shrewd green gaze, panic flaring in my stomach for a moment before she gives me her gorgeous smile and takes a sip of her drink. I sit back in my seat, soaking up the joy and happiness that fills the car. It's like I can finally take a deep breath after drowning for so long, and I've surfaced to find myself on a tropical island, the hot sun shining down on me.

The song finishes and *Beautiful Girls* by Sean Kingston comes on, accompanied by girlish squeals from the others. Anastasia half gets up and starts to do an impressive body roll, her gold dress twinkling in the lights. We soon pull up to a stop, and the door next to Lexi opens, letting in a rush of cold autumn air.

"Thanks, Tony," I hear her sensual voice say, but I miss his gruff reply.

I'm the last to get out, and they're all waiting for me with excitement in their gazes. A tingle of nervous anticipation races through me as I look up at the old, light coloured stone building.

There's nothing on the outside to suggest it's a restaurant or a business of any sort. It's an end of terrace townhouse, with steps leading up to a huge, shiny black front door. A black metal railing borders the front with neat box hedging behind it and a spiral metal staircase leading down to, presumably, the basement level. It's three stories high, with high windows facing the street, all with curtains drawn.

"Is this Grey's? I thought it was a restaurant." I comment, confused, and eliciting a chorus of feminine giggles as I continue gazing up at it.

"Yep, this is Grey's," Lexi replies, with amusement in her tone.

"So, it's not a restaurant then?" I ask, looking at her warily. She bursts out laughing, the sound wrapping around me like silk.

"No," she tells me, still chuckling as they lead me around to the side of the building where I can see another shiny black door. "It's a club, sugarplum," she says before turning to rap her knuckles on the door. "Open up, buttercup!"

A club? I think as the door swings open, and there's a guy in a suit standing in the doorway. He's built like a brick shit house! He's huge, taking up almost the entire space. I'm surprised that he could even get a suit in his size, although by the looks of it, I wouldn't be surprised to learn it was made in Savile Row, where the best tailors in England have their shops.

"Evening, Lexi," he greets her, and I can't help the shiver that tingles across me. His voice is like warm whiskey on cold nights. He steps back, nodding at the others as they pass. I go to step in and find my way blocked by his massive bulk.

"This is Laura. She's with us, Ryan," Lexi assures him, stepping forward and placing a manicured hand on his enormous bicep.

I look up into his eyes, noticing that they're a beautiful hazelnut brown colour. His brows are drawn down, assessing me, and I can't help the hitch in my breath as he takes me in. Something softens in his eyes before he steps aside. As I pass, I smile my thanks, able to see him in the light better. His chestnut hair is buzzed short on the sides and slightly longer on top, and I can just see tattoos peeking from under his collar.

"Thank you, Ryan," I say softly, captured in his gaze once more.

He nods, then I see his gaze slip down to my neck, eyes hardening like sharp stones. Before he can say anything, Lexi grabs my arm and tugs me away.

"Looks like you've already got yourself a fan, gorgeous," she whispers conspiratorially in my ear.

"What?!" I choke out.

"He can't take his eyes off you, girl," Coco adds from in front of me, and I glance back to see Ryan looking after me intensely. I shake my head at them and scoff.

We come to another doorway that is opened at our approach, a second big suited guy behind it. Stepping through, I see that we're in a lobby of sorts. It's gently lit with a chandelier and wall lights, the floor covered in black and white tiles. The walls are painted a soft grey, and I can see a dark wooden staircase against one wall, leading to what I assume are the upper levels.

It still doesn't look much like a club to me, but then I guess I've had little experience of anything like that. I only went out with Ace to places that he approved, so I've never actually been in a club, but I did imagine them to be louder.

There's a dark wood reception desk with a very smartly dressed blonde receptionist behind it, who smiles warmly at our approach.

"Good evening, ladies," she grins. She's incredibly well-spoken, like a newsreader.

"Hi, Sami," Anastasia says, her voice definitely has a Russian lilt to it.

"And who is this?" Sami questions, turning her blue eyes to me.

"I'm Laura," I reply, feeling slightly bolder after having met so many new people tonight.

"Pleasure to meet you, Laura," she replies warmly, and I can't help but smile back.

"Is Grey upstairs?" Lexi asks, stepping up to us.

"Yes, he is. Shall I call up to let him know you're back?" Sami enquires.

"Tell him I'm on my way up," Lexi orders as she grabs my hand and leads me towards the wide staircase.

I hear Sami's voice speak softly into the phone as we make our way up. The stairs have a thick, plush Persian rug running down the middle of them, and my boot-clad feet sink in with every step. This place screams exclusivity and money with its tasteful gentlemen's club vibe. *What kind of club is this exactly?*

We reach the first floor, and a faint whiff of cigar smoke tickles my nose before Lexi is dragging me up the next flight. The walls are still painted the same soft grey colour, but there's no panelling up here, just the dark wood of the stairs. We come to the final landing, which has three dark wood doors coming off of it. This must have been the old servants' quarters.

Lexi strides up to the door opposite the staircase, knocking on the panelled wooden door.

"Come in, Lexi," a deep voice commands, and a shiver runs through me at the sound.

Lexi opens the door, walking in as if the voice doesn't affect her at all. I follow behind, slightly more reticent. The room we're in is large, with a fairly high ceiling that slopes at the sides like this was once the attic. It's painted a darker grey than the hallway, but it doesn't feel cold. There's even a small fireplace with a cheerful fire burning behind the grate.

"Ah, you must be Laura," the deep voice sounds from across the room, and my gaze catches the grey eyes of a man sitting in a leather wing-back chair behind a dark wooden desk. There are two smaller leather chairs in front of it, both unoccupied.

He's exceptionally handsome, with classical features, salt and pepper hair that's slicked back, and is wearing a dark charcoal grey suit, a white shirt, and silver tie. There's a twinkle in the tie, which looks like a diamond tie pin. He stands up and comes around to our side of the desk, and I can see that the suit is tailored to perfection, fitting his lean form perfectly.

He holds out a hand, a warm smile drawing up the corners of his mouth.

"I'm Grey, and it's a pleasure to make your acquaintance," he assures me in cultured tones.

I take his hand and discover it's warm and dry, not sweaty, and he gives a firm but not overbearing handshake before releasing his grip.

"Shall we?" he asks, indicating to the chairs, and we all take a seat, myself and Lexi in front of the desk and Grey behind it.

"Can I get you something to drink, Laura? Lexi?" he asks us politely.

"No, thank you," I smile weakly at him, butterflies dancing in my stomach.

"No thanks, Grey darling," Lexi answers with a cheeky grin.

"Now," he smiles warmly at me, and I feel a sense of safety around him that confuses me. "How can I help you, Laura?"

Before I can say anything, Lexi butts in. "Laura is going to be our new waitress, and she'll be staying with me." Grey doesn't say anything, just raises a perfect dark brow and smiles indulgently at her.

"I see," he replies.

"If-if that's okay with you?" I stutter out, cursing my new nervousness.

"Do you know what type of establishment this is, Laura?" he asks me, not answering my question. I shake my head in response. "Well, we are an exclusive gentlemen's club that caters to our members' *needs*."

I nod, thinking that to be the case from what I've seen so far.

"I take care of all my girls, no one is forced to do anything they are unhappy with, but there are opportunities for those who want them." He continues, gesturing with his hand. "Can I suggest that Lexi show you around tonight, then you can start a trial run tomorrow, provided you're happy to do so, of course?"

"That would be wonderful, thank you," I reply, tears stinging my eyes at my good fortune.

"Excellent," he grins. "Lexi, I'd like to have a word with Laura alone. Please wait outside." And all of a sudden, the butterflies are back.

"Before I go, Kol was at Maxine's." She tells him, and the skin around his eyes tightens slightly, the only indication of his displeasure. He gives her a sharp nod.

Lexi squeezes my arm reassuringly before getting up and leaving, closing the door quietly behind her.

"I don't expect you to tell me who left those bruises on your neck, trust needs to be earned, after all. But know that if you ever need whoever it was taken care of, you just say the word." He is absolutely serious, eyes boring into mine until I nod, and then he smiles kindly at me.

"As I said, I take care of my girls," he reiterates.

"Thank you," I whisper, meaning it. How can a stranger show such kindness when my own family couldn't care less?

"Now, go with Lexi, have a look around, then get some sleep.

Tomorrow, you can go to the tailors and get your uniform, then start tomorrow evening," he tells me, and I feel my head already beginning to spin with a mixture of relief, and the speed at which this is all progressing.

Nodding again, I'm like one of those nodding dogs people put in the back of their cars at this stage, I get up and head towards the door.

"Oh, and Laura?" I hear him say behind me, and I turn to look at him. "Welcome to Grey's."

CHAPTER FIVE

I wake up with a start, sweat covering my trembling body as I sit up looking frantically around the darkened room. It takes me a beat, but then I remember where I am; Lexi's house, spare bedroom, North London.

Taking a few deep breaths, I try to calm my racing heart as I remember everything that happened yesterday. The cafe, meeting Lexi and the girls, Grey's, looking around the club...I put my head in my hands with a groan as I remember the tour of Grey's.

As Lexi describes it, it's a gentlemen's club with strippers. Super exclusive, members are invite only, and anyone stepping out of line finds themselves out on their arse sharpish. It's where people take business associates, people who they want to impress, but you basically have to be in the top one percent to gain an invitation. A moment of worry flashes through me, the thought that Ace or any one of the founding members of Black Knight Corporation could potentially walk through the doors.

The door swings open, startling me out of my thoughts, and Lexi bounds in wearing short shorts and a vest top that does nothing to support her ample tits. She leaps on the bed with a squeal, bouncing her boobs up and down.

"Good morning, sunshine!" She shrieks with excitement, and I can't help but laugh in return. It's amazing to think that I've never really had a close female friend before. I didn't know what I was missing!

"Good morning," I smile back and feel lighter and full of hope this morning. Like things may finally be going alright.

"So, we've got breakfast first, then Schmidt's, then I thought we could go shopping!" she lists off excitedly.

"What's Schmidt's?" I ask, my brow furrowing.

"Why, the tailor for your uniform, silly!" she replies, smacking me lightly on the arm.

"Oh," my heart sinks. I can't afford to waste money on a tailored uniform, or go shopping. Although, I suppose window shopping would be okay.

"Don't look like that! Grey pays for the expenses, dummy! And the uniform is an expense," she shakes her head like I'm an imbecile.

"Oh," I say again, like a broken record.

"So, come on! Get your arse out of bed and into the shower!" She pushes me until I almost tumble out of bed, catching myself just in time. Straightening up, I go to walk towards the bathroom when a crack lands on my bum making me shout out.

"Get a move on, slowpoke!" she shouts while laughing. Rubbing my sore buttcheek, I chuckle to myself as I head out of the bedroom door.

Lexi's riverside apartment really is gorgeous. It's a modern open plan affair, with two bedrooms and a huge bathroom, plus stunning views overlooking the River Thames and the city. Apparently, Grey owns the entire building and houses all his girls here, like one big sorority house.

As we exit the building, I notice there's a black SUV with that same smoke motif waiting for us. I shiver as the wind whistles around me, the day overcast and grey. Lexi said we wouldn't need coats, but I'm regretting my choice of a loose long-sleeved dress, and cardigan with tights, and flat knee-high boots.

We climb into the back, Lexi saying hello to our driver, Sean. It really surprises me how much Grey takes care of his girls, and I can't help the fissure of worry that sparks inside of me.

"Just spit it out, Laura," Lexi demands in a joking, exasperated tone when she notices my worries.

I decided to just bite the bullet. "Is Grey your pimp?"

She chokes with laughter, her whole face going red. I even hear gruff chuckles coming from Sean up front.

"Our pimp?!" She pats my leg condescendingly. "No dearest, Grey is not our pimp." She wipes under her eyes, checking for smudged makeup. She looks particularly stunning in a deep green Ralph Lauren wrap dress.

"So, what's this all about?" I ask, indicating the car, the apartment, and the expenses.

"He likes to take care of us. That's it. No hidden agenda, no surprise cost," she tells me, and I can see the admiration in her eyes. "Rumour has it that something happened to his mother when he was younger, and he vowed that he'd look after any woman from that day on," she tells me dreamily.

Sean scoffs from the front. "They also say his cock is made from twenty-four karat gold, so I wouldn't go believing everything you hear."

"Sean!" Lexi scolds him, but I can see the laughter in her eyes.

Shortly after, we pull up outside a sweet little café, and I can see we've reached Savile Row by the black and white street sign on the side of the building.

"Breakfast, m'dear," Lexi explains proudly as we get out of the car. Sean assures us he'll park nearby, so we just have to call when we're done.

The café is beautiful, with a red awning and plants tumbling from pots and window boxes. There's a burgundy sign that reads Brushh in gold letters and several tables are outside. But as it's grey and looks like it could rain, something I haven't missed about England, we decide to sit inside.

As soon as we open the door, a gust of wind comes in with us, and I'm hit by the wonderful smell of freshly baked bread and other baked goodies.

"Maxine makes the best pastries in London," Lexi tells me, and I must say by smell alone I think she might be right.

"Ah, Lexi! So good to see you! And who's your beautiful new friend?" A short lady bustles over to us. Her accent is most definitely French, and I can feel a blush spread across my cheeks at the compliment.

"Maxine, this is Laura. She starts at Grey's today, and this is her first day in London so I knew where we had to go for breakfast!"

"Well, welcome, Laura!" Maxine beams at me and hustles us over to a table near the window. "Shall I bring two continental specials?" she asks.

"Yes please, love. And two juices of the day as well." Lexi orders for both of us. It should irk me; Ace would order for me all the time and dictate what I could eat and even how much I could eat. But it's different with Lexi. I know she's just doing it out of kindness, not control. Maxine smiles kindly and heads back the way she came, presumably to sort our order.

"So," Lexi turns her intelligent green gaze to me, and by the twinkle in her eyes, I know that she's up to no good. My heart races, I'm not ready to talk about my past yet. "What did you think of Ryan?"

"Ryan?!" I splutter out. I didn't see that coming. "What about him?" I ask, heat warming my cheeks once more.

"Oh come on, Laura! I saw him checking you out last night at the club. He couldn't take his eyes off of you, and he was meant to man the side door but swapped so that he could keep looking," she informs me with a smirk. "And, he has that whole delicious protective Alpha vibe about him."

I busy my hands with a napkin, tearing small pieces off of it. My mother would be horrified at my bad manners.

"Ryan is very attractive, but, well, I'm not after anything like that at the moment," I reply, my gaze darting up to hers and seeing that damn smirk on her lips.

"Uh-huh," she mumbles, unconvinced.

Luckily, I'm saved from further conversation by Maxine bringing over our drinks. Taking a long slurp through the straw, I'm hit with the fresh taste of oranges, apples, carrots, and a hint of ginger. It instantly wakes me up and refreshes me.

Lexi seems to get that I'd rather not talk about it and talks for the rest of breakfast, telling me all about her less than stellar upbringing on a rough council estate before Grey discovered her and offered her a job at the club. He really does sound like a Knight in shining armour, or perhaps slightly tarnished armour given the fact that fundamentally he owns a strip club and lord knows what else. He must have his fingers in many pies to be able to spend what he seems to.

After breakfast, we walked down the road to Schmidt's Tailors. The shop looks exactly how I remember a Savile Row tailor to look; a wooden counter with lots of drawers behind a curtained off portion, and presumably a backroom or upper floor where the clothes are made.

As we enter, a wizened old man approaches us looking rather stern. He has on a grey waistcoat with a shirt and tie and dress trousers. Around his elbows are those things that they used to wear in the fifties to keep their sleeves in place. There's a tape measure dangling around his neck.

"This way," he commands in a rough voice, indicating the curtained off area. I look at Lexi who leans in.

"That's Schmidt. He's a little rough around the edges, but he's the best," she whispers.

I follow him, stepping through the drawn red velvet curtains into a space that is almost entirely surrounded by mirrors. There's a woman waiting with what looks like some garments already half made over one arm. She must be in her late forties, with mid-brown hair and kind brown eyes. She smiles warmly at me, and my lips lift in return. "Undress," Schmidt orders, and I baulk at the command, remembering the bruises that decorate my body.

"It's okay, Laura," Lexi says softly behind me.

I take in a deep breath, deciding that I won't be ashamed of what I've been through. Remembering that what doesn't kill you only makes you stronger as they say. I take my clothes off, straightening up, and cringe at the sight I'm confronted with in the mirrors. My body is a watercolour of purples, greens, and yellows, littered with the remains of Ace's violence, and I'm thin to the point of being able to see the outlines of my ribs. I used to be quite curvy, but Ace thought I was fat so he put me on a strict diet.

I hear a sharp intake of breath and look up to see the pitying gaze of the woman holding the garments before she can school her features. My eyes meet Lexi's in the mirror. She gives me a sad smile, but there is no pity in her gaze. It's the look of shared experience, of someone who's been there and gotten out. It gives me the strength to stand a little taller and face my demons staring back at me.

CHAPTER SIX

We arrive back at Lexi's with so many bags I've lost count. Poor Sean even had to carry some up to the apartment for us. Apparently, according to Lexi, I needed a lot of new clothes, so after Schmidt's, we headed west to Oxford Street and spent a small fortune there as well, which also counts as expenses according to Lexi. She whipped out a Grey's company card no less, so she must know what she's talking about.

It's late afternoon, so we basically have to dump our bags and head straight to Grey's for my training before the evening begins.

Pulling up outside of the club, it looks even more inconspicuous in the daylight, just like any other building on what appears to be a residential street. We head to the side door, and once again, Ryan opens it; his eyes go straight past Lexi to lock with mine.

"Good afternoon, Laura," he says in that deliciously deep voice of his.

"G-good afternoon, Ryan," I stutter back, blushing furiously.

"Good afternoon, Ryan," Lexi teases him, smirking when he squirms a little, realising that he totally ignored her.

"Hi, Lexi," he replies, and his cheeks flush.

"Can we come in, or are you gonna make us stand out on the street all night?" she sasses back, and he hurriedly moves aside, stumbling out an apology.

She links her arm through mine, pulling me inside and leaning her head so close I can smell her expensive perfume. "Oh girl, he's got it bad," she laughs, and I look back to see Ryan still looking after me, an intense look in his brown eyes.

My heart does a little flutter, which is promptly squashed by guilt. I left Tom behind not a week ago, and here I am starting to crush on another guy. Never mind the fact that I'm pregnant! A bubble of worry is added to the guilt at that thought. I won't be able to hide my pregnancy forever, and then what will I do?

I just can't worry about that right now, I think to myself, shaking my head. We continue on to a side room that's been set aside as a dressing room of sorts for all of the girls. This, too, is guarded at all times by a burly security guy who nods at our approach. Stepping inside, we're engulfed by feminine chatter and a cloud of different perfumes all merging together in an overwhelming fog.

"Ladies!" I hear the camp tones of Justin, to whom I was introduced to last night, call out and see him hurrying towards us. He's Grey's dresser and sources all the costumes and anything else that Grey's girls need whilst they're here.

He air kisses both of us, and I take in his outfit. He's wearing a sharp collared floral shirt, a silk scarf, fitted trousers, and killer black patent heels. His straw-coloured blond hair is styled to perfection in a quiff, and he has a wonderful moustache that he curls upwards so that, with his goatee, he looks like the character from the KFC adverts.

"Lexi darling, I've laid the Westwood red sequins out for you tonight," he tells her, shooing her over to her dressing table, rail, and mirror. Yep, that's right, Vivienne Westwood designs all the girl's outfits.

"Laura, Schmidt just delivered your uniform so chop chop!"

He rushes me over to an empty dressing table where I can see a rail with a white shirt, grey pencil skirt, and grey fitted waistcoat hanging.

There's a pair of shiny black heels resting on the floor next to the rail, and as I approach, I see that they're Jimmy Choo brand. No expense spared, I guess. On the table is a push-up red lace bra, matching thong and suspender belt, and sheer stockings with a seam running up the back of them.

He stands by whilst I get changed, not batting an eye at the bruises that I expose for the second time today. He does help me clip the back of the stockings in place but leaves me to wiggle into the pencil skirt. Luckily, the back has a modest split, otherwise, I'm not sure I'd be able to walk in it. Slipping my feet into the heels, grateful that I'm used to wearing ones of a similar height, I straighten up to see a frown marring his brow.

"What?" I ask, looking into the floor-length mirror on the wall beside me. The bra has made the most of my bust and combined with the skirt and fitted waistcoat, I look like I've got more of an hourglass figure than I actually have. My eyes float to my neck, and I see what Justin's problem is. There's a ring of purple bruises that look exactly like what they are; fingerprints.

As I'm staring at my reflection, I see Justin whip off his colourful silk scarf, then he wraps it around my neck a couple of times and ties a little knot to one side. I look like a fifties air hostess, but it's pretty hot if I do say so myself.

"There," he says with a nod and a smile before his attention is caught by one of the others, and he rushes off to help her.

I gaze at my reflection once more, amazed at the girl staring back at me. She looks confident and beautiful, with her stunning figure and made up face, and you'd never know that just days ago she was in a place far away and full of darkness.

"Stop admiring your beautiful arse, and let's show you the ropes!" Lexi calls out from the other side of the room.

Courage, I tell myself, taking a deep breath and heading into the unknown.

Hours later, I throw myself down on my bed with a whoosh of breath. I don't even know what time it is, two maybe three AM? It's late, or I suppose early depending on how you look at it, and I'm cream crackered!

The night was...interesting? Eye opening? It was both and so much more. The bar work wasn't difficult, taking orders down in the basement, then going to the bar at the back and bringing the drinks to the tables. Each table has a pole and is surrounded by four dark leather wing-back chairs so each table has a dancer.

And the girls are phenomenal dancers...who happen to take their clothes off. There are women of every race, colour, and dancing to suit every taste. Interestingly, many of the patrons, or members, seemed more interested in talking with each other than ogling the girls. They're great tippers at least. I don't know what the girls made tonight, but I must have made around five hundred pounds in tips.

They were all on their best behaviour, no touching allowed. That is unless you get a private room upstairs, then a contract is written, dictating any boundaries and signed by all parties. There's also a smoking lounge on the upper floors and another bar that I may work at some nights.

My first night flew by, and before I knew it, Lexi and I were being driven back by Sean to Lexi's riverside apartment. After taking a quick shower, I'm snuggled in the comfy bed, my eyelids drooping, yet my mind whirling with all that has happened over the past few days.

I can't believe how different my life is in such a short space of time. I never dreamed that not only would I break free from Ace and his toxic hold, but I'd find friends for the first time in my life. The girls are all so nice, especially Lexi, and I can see myself being happy here.

A bubble of anxiety bursts in my stomach. I've no idea what I'll do once I start showing. I mean, I doubt they'd want a pregnant waitress, and I've never heard of a pregnant stripper, or if that would even be an option?

Stop it! Stop worrying about what is yet to come! I internally scold myself. One day at a time.

CHAPTER SEVEN

A few weeks pass with the same tiring routine. Waitressing at the club in the evening, sleeping most of the day, and getting up at lunchtime. Often myself, Lexi, and some of the other girls go into town, Lexi insisting that she show me the sights of London. I don't have the heart to tell her I've seen many of them before, and anyway, going with her and the others is like seeing London for the first time. They all have such life and vitality about them, it's as if I'm waking up from a deep slumber and seeing the world in all its technicolour.

Luckily, I've not suffered from any morning sickness, although I've had a couple of episodes of vomiting that I managed to easily explain away. What I can't do anything about is the tightness of my high-waisted uniform skirt around my middle. It's becoming more obvious that I'm getting bigger, and I've finally gotten my curvy figure back. Although I have put on weight by eating properly for the first time in years, it can't explain the roundness of my stomach.

One evening, just before I'm due to start, Sami tells me that Grey would like a word with me in his office. I can't stop the nervous butterflies that flutter in my stomach as I climb the stairs to the top floor. Or they could be my baby, I'm sure I've started feeling it move a bit.

Reaching the upper landing, I stop outside his door, knocking lightly.

"Come in, Laura," his deep voice invites me in from the other side, and I open the door to find Grey sitting behind his desk smiling warmly at me. Lexi is also in the room, and I feel myself hesitate as my flight mode kicks in.

"Please take a seat, Laura," Grey gestures to the other empty chair next to Lexi, taking away my decision to flee with the kind way he makes the order almost a request.

I can feel my chest rising and falling with shallow pants as I sit on the edge of the chair, looking down at my hands which are wringing in my lap. Lexi's hand reaches over to grab one of mine, stilling the movement and giving it a reassuring squeeze.

"You're not in any trouble, gorgeous, no one is angry," she assures me softly, ducking her head and catching my gaze, giving me a smile.

"Lexi is right, Laura, please don't worry. You're not in any kind of trouble. We just want to help," Grey says kindly, making me look up at him.

"O-okay," I stammer out, trying to calm my racing heart by taking deeper breaths.

"Am I correct in assuming that there will be a happy occasion in a few months' time?" he asks gently. There's genuine warmth in his eyes, and it gives me the courage to nod my head in confirmation. "Congratulations my dear, what wonderful news." He beams at me, his handsome face becoming even more devastating than before.

Tears prick my eyes as my breath rushes out of me in relief. Lexi squeezes my hand again, and I look into her green eyes only to see a touch of excitement there as well as happiness.

"Do you know how far along you are, babe?" she asks me.

"Um, maybe about three months, I think. I've just started feeling flutterings."

"Well, may I suggest we get you seen by someone as soon as

possible to check you and baby over and get a scan?" Grey proposes in his business-like manner. "I know an excellent consultant and midwife on Harley Street who I can call in the morning."

"Oh, um, I'm sure I can see a local doctor. I don't want to be a bother."

"Nonsense." he assures me. "I told you before that I look after my girls, and I meant it."

"Your girls? I thought once you..." I trail off when I see him shake his head grinning, like I'm amusing him.

"You thought that when I found out, I would terminate your employment?" he asks kindheartedly.

"You're not?" I'm so confused. *Why wouldn't he?*

"No, Laura. I'm not going to terminate your contract. Although, I can't have you serving drinks in your condition, especially with the stairs," he tells me, and I nod, still a little puzzled as to what exactly I'll be doing.

"Have you ever considered dancing, Laura?" he asks, fingers steepled.

"Dancing?" I repeat, still none the wiser.

"Like Lexi and the others do," he prompts me, and I just sit and stare at him.

"But...I'm pregnant! Surely no one would want to see a pregnant stripper?" I question. *He can't be serious, can he?*

"On the contrary, my dear. A great many men find pregnant women incredibly attractive. It's a primal urge. You see, many men will seek out women who are fertile, it's an evolutionary tactic, and none are more so than a woman who is already carrying a child," he informs me, and I must confess I'm in shock. I had no idea this was even a thing men would find so attractive.

"You don't need to decide right now, take time to think about it. And be assured that I'm having a maternity package drawn up as we speak so that you can have plenty of time off to prepare before and after the baby arrives," he says, and my head reels.

I'm lost for words. I can't find any to express my delighted surprise at this turn of events.

"Excellent. Now, take the night off. I'll have Ryan drive you back so you have time to think. Let me know what you decide, say in a week, but Laura," he looks at me seriously, "there's no pressure if you don't want to dance. We will find something else for you to do."

"Th-thank you," I say around the lump in my throat. Getting up, I head towards the door with Lexi by my side.

My mind swirls with questions. *Would I want to dance like Lexi and the others? Take my clothes off for men to admire my body. My changing body? I'm not sure I would want that. Yet, why am I a little excited by the thought?*

I step out into the brisk evening breeze, wrapping my coat around myself. It's late October, and it's gotten chilly with the dropping temperature. It's getting darker earlier too, and winter is definitely on the way.

Shivering, I walk over to the waiting black SUV, and get into the passenger side, figuring there's no point sitting in the back by myself when I could sit next to Ryan.

Over the last few weeks, I've noticed him. A lot. He's always watching me, not in a creepy way, but like he can't take his eyes off of me. It's intoxicating and makes my cheeks burn. I can't help seeking him out if he's nearby, and the small smiles he gives me set my heart racing in my chest.

At the same time, I feel guilty. I left Tom behind, and I can't help but feel like I'm cheating on him somehow, even though it's unlikely we will see each other again. I loved him, still love him. So how can I also have feelings for Ryan? *You can't love more than one person at a time, right?*

"Penny for your thoughts?" his gruff voice sounds, breaking me out of my confused thoughts.

"Oh," I reply, flushing and squirming at the question, my hands fidgeting in my lap. "Um, well, I was considering an offer that Grey made me."

"And what was that?" He growls, and I look up to see his hands tighten on the steering wheel and his jaw clenched.

"Well, he suggested that I might consider becoming a dancer at the club," I admit, watching for his reaction.

"Will you?" he asks, brown eyes flickering to me then back to the road. I can't read his facial expression, whether he's happy or angry at the suggestion. And that bothers me. I realise with a start that I want to know what he thinks, whether he approves or not. This desire for his approval bothers me. I've had a lifetime of pleasing others at my own expense, yet I still wanted to do just that for him. "There's good money to be made in tips, so the girls tell me," he adds.

"I hadn't really considered it before now, however, I think there must be something freeing about taking your clothes off and being watched like that," I tell him, and his brows dip in confusion.

"How so?" he enquires, like he's genuinely interested in what I've got to say.

"Well, society expects women to cover up, to conform to certain standards. To be beautiful but not vain, to be admired but not to revel in it. Getting up on a table and taking your clothes off for the sole purpose to be, well, worshipped and to have your body lusted after, it's kind of like a big F-you to society and its rules. Don't you think?" I ask back, not realising that I actually felt so strongly about it. Although, it's not surprising given the way my parents and then Ace tried to repress me and force me to conform to their ideals.

I look at Ryan as we pull up outside mine and Lexi's building and can see that he's really considering what I've just said.

"I've never thought about it like that before," he tells me, "but I guess you're right. I don't look down on any girl who dances, it's nothing to be ashamed of."

He brings the car to a stop and parks while we sit there for a minute in silence.

"So, are you going to dance?" he asks me, his tone curious but not judgemental as he turns the full weight of his chocolate brown gaze onto me.

"I don't know. I mean, I didn't think it would be an option considering..." I trail off, realising that he's going to find out sooner or later but not quite able to make myself say it.

"Considering?" he queries with a raised brow, and I take a deep breath.

"Considering I'm pregnant," I say, staring him straight in the eye like I'm ripping a plaster off. Both his brows go up, his eyes falling straight to my stomach as he chews on his full bottom lip in the most distracting way.

"Ah," he starts, releasing his lip. "And Grey knows and wants you to dance anyway?" he questions me, and I nod in confirmation. "Well, pregnant birds are hot as hell," he mutters, and I can't help the bubble of laughter that escapes my lips.

"That's what Grey said," I chuckle, and he smiles in return. It's a smile so full of warmth that I can almost feel it seep into my skin, heating me from the inside out until it feels like the sun is inside me. *Damn, he really is pretty.*

"Would you like to come up?" I offer. "You know, if you don't have to rush back?"

"I'd love to," he responds, his blinding smile firmly in place as he switches the engine off.

We get out and head up to the apartment, the chilly night surrounding us as we walk towards the building. We're both quiet as we get the lift up to Lexi's floor, and it's only then do I realise how awkward things are between us. It's like I've invited him up for coffee, which I guess I have, but you know, like *coffee*. As in, well, sex. Or, maybe, just making out? *Gah! Even my brain is nervous rambling.*

"So, the weather has gotten colder recently..." I start, wanting to smack my hands over my face. *The weather?! Really?!*

He lets out a deep rumbling laugh that helps break the tension.

"That was..." I say cringing.

"Terrible?" he spits out in between bouts of laughter, and this time I join in with him.

The lift pings our floor, and the doors open. It's a short walk down the hallway; there are only maybe five apartments on each floor. Letting myself in using the spare key that Lexi gave me, I turn on the lights. Ryan follows behind me, closing the door softly and cocooning us in the quiet.

I turn around to offer him, well, coffee or something, but end up finding him standing so close that I'm enveloped in his comforting scent. He smells like cardamom and spicy cinnamon, like safety and warmth and comfort. My breath catches on an inhale, trying to keep his scent inside of me. His hand reaches out to brush my now red hair behind my ear.

"I want to kiss you so badly, Laura," he rasps out, and a shiver travels over my body at his words. I desperately want him to place his lips on mine, I ache with the need to feel them against me. It may be pregnancy hormones or sheer attraction, but it's taking everything inside of me to hold back in this moment.

"I-I can't get into anything serious, Ryan," I tell him, closing my eyes as his fingertips glide down the side of my face. I feel a warmth along the front of me and raise my eyelids to see that he's stepped up to me and is so close my breasts are brushing his hard chest. "But I need..."

"What do you need, baby?" he asks me quietly, cupping my jaw and tilting my head so that I'm looking up at him. My cheeks flush at what I want to say, and a knowing sexy as sin smirk crosses his lips.

"Oh baby, I've got you," he croons, lowering his lips until they are brushing against mine. A needy moan escapes me at the light caress. "Nothing serious," he states right before he closes the distance.

Our kiss starts off slow, an exploration of each other's mouths and tongues. It quickly turns heated, burning, as weeks of pent up attraction come to the surface. He strips off my coat, and I do the same to him, marvelling at how hot his body is. I can feel his body heat through his shirt.

His hands tangle in my hair as he guides me backwards until the backs of my knees hit the leather sofa. He breaks our kiss to gently push me back until I'm sitting down and looking up at him. There's a fire in his eyes that burns me from the inside out, and he's panting, his chest heaving. He gives me another devastatingly sexy grin and he undoes his tie, throwing it aside, and unbuttoning his white shirt. As the fabric parts, it reveals dark tattoos covering his entire ripped torso, starting at his collarbone and disappearing into his suit trousers, which have a definite bulge in them.

I gasp audibly as he pushes the shirt down his arms, and I see that the beautiful drawings on his skin go all the way down to his cuffs. They are in a kaleidoscope of colours, like a beautiful rainbow, chasing across his body. Looking back up into his face, I see he has a self-assured grin on his lush lips. I like this side of him, this confident swagger. He toes his shoes off, kicking them to one side as he kneels down in front of me.

Grabbing one of my legs, he slowly unzips my knee-high leather boot, pulling it off before doing the same to the other one. He reaches underneath my checkered miniskirt, grabs the waistband of my tights and knickers, and pulls them over my hips and off my legs. My heart is racing, my breaths shallow as his fingertips brushing over me leave trails of fire in his wake. Grabbing behind my knees, he pulls me to the edge of the sofa and spreads my thighs wide. He growls in appreciation when he sees how wet I am for him, licking his lips as he moves his head towards my core.

I'm panting, my chest rising and falling rapidly with each breath as his head disappears underneath my skirt. I feel his hot tongue on my inner folds, and I almost come off the sofa. I would have too had his arm not clamped down across my hips, holding me into place. It feels incredible, tingles of pleasure racing across my whole body as his tongue works me like I'm his last meal on earth and he's savouring every mouthful. My head tips back with a guttural groan as the pleasure starts to build to a crescendo, lightning racing across my skin.

"Ryan," I gasp as he picks up speed, sucking and nibbling my clit.

Two fingers tease my entrance, coating themselves in my juices before they push inside me and start fucking me, hitting my G-spot every time. My climax crashes over me like a wave as I scream out his name and grip the leather of the sofa tightly.

When I open my eyes, it's to see him looking up at me from his kneeling position, his chin glistening with my release and a satisfied smirk on his face. Bracing his hands on my knees, he leans up and into me, kissing me hard, and I can taste myself on his tongue.

"Perhaps we should take this to your bedroom?" he asks, pulling back. I nod, unable to form words.

He picks me up under my thighs, giving me a second to wrap my arms around his neck and my legs around his waist as he stands up, taking me with him. My bare, wet pussy touches his hot skin, and I groan at the contact, grinding into his hard abs and creating a delicious friction. He growls at me, nipping my neck and heading towards the only hallway in the place.

"The last on the right," I manage to croak out.

Somehow, he is able to use one hand to open the door, kicking it shut behind him and striding across to my bed. He places me down onto it, before straightening up, his hands going to his belt. My eyes rapturously follow his movements as he undoes the buckle, then the button, and finally the fly on his trousers. He pushes them over his hips, along with whatever underwear he's wearing, and steps out of them. I take a sharp breath at the sight before me.

He is simply huge, hung like a horse! And I had no idea you could get a tattoo, well, *there*. Across his upper thigh and hip is a stunning Japanese style scene, with rolling blue-grey clouds, and floating pink cherry blossoms. This beautiful artwork extends over his balls, and up onto the other hip, interspersed with red peonies. Above his impressive length is a green double-headed dragon, one head looking up towards his torso, and the other...the other is *his* head. Like his dick. His cock is tattooed completely, from base to tip, his tip being the second dragon head! He's clean shaven down there, so the picture is completely uninterrupted.

"Like what you see, baby?" his gruff voice asks, sounding amused and pleased at the same time.

"Um...I'm not sure you'll fit!" I blurt out, then clap my hands over my traitorous mouth. *Hello! Brain to mouth filter, anyone there?*

"Oh trust me, baby, it'll fit." A deep chuckle sounds from between his kissed swollen lips. I see him reach down to the floor, taking his wallet out of his trouser pocket, and pulling out a foil packet. He opens it, rolling the condom on with ease which surprises me a little given his size. *Maybe he buys extra large ones?* He kneels onto the bed, crawling towards me with a wicked look in his eyes.

"You are wearing too many clothes, Miss Darling," he informs me, reaching out to unzip my skirt and pull it down off my hips. My black long-sleeved top is next, and I'm so grateful that all the bruises have long faded. I'm sure he's heard the rumours that have no doubt spread around the club, but at least he won't see the evidence. I can't help feeling a twinge of shame that I let someone do that to me for so long. I know it's not my fault, but I'm starting to slowly realise that I am worth more than someone's fists. I deserve so much more, and it took getting pregnant for me to see this. Ryan then takes off my soft bra, I can't stand to wear normal bras at the moment, my breasts are just too tender.

Once we are both naked, he gently pushes me down until I'm lying before him. He's still kneeling above me on the bed and looking down at me with such desire that I feel the flush spread over my skin. I've always been quick to blush.

"You are so beautiful, Laura," he tells me, admiration clear in his voice. His hands reach out and gently caress my slightly rounded stomach in reverence.

"It doesn't bother you?" I ask him, curious but suddenly worried that it will.

"Far from it," he tells me softly, still stroking my abdomen, sending tingles across my skin.

His gaze meets mine, and I see the truth in his words. He really doesn't care that I'm carrying another man's child. He leans down over me, capturing my lips with his as he settles in between my legs, his tip nudging my slick opening.

"You tell me if you want to stop or if anything is uncomfortable, okay?" he asks and waits for my nod before he starts to push inside of me.

My hands come up and grip his shoulders, the stretch of him entering me is so exquisite I can't stop the deep moan that leaves my lips.

"Shit, Laura," he growls out as he finally bottoms out, fully seated deep inside of me. He's up on his elbows, and he uses the leverage to slowly pump in and out, gyrating his hips so that he's massaging my clit too.

"Ryan! Yes!" I rasp out as he picks up speed, sending blissful tendrils of pleasure shooting all over my body.

"Laura, you feel. So. Fucking. Good," he groans out, every word punctuated with a thrust of his hips until he's practically slamming into me. I tip over the edge, falling into another mind shattering orgasm, and I hear him cry out his own release moments later.

He rolls off me, pulling me in his arms so that my head is resting on his sweat covered chest. It rises and falls with his panting breaths, and I can feel his heartbeat racing like my own as we both come down from our high.

"Feeling better, baby?" he asks me, and I can hear the smile in his voice.

"Much, thank you," I reply primly, then burst out laughing. He huffs out a chuckle too, and we lie there wrapped in each other's arms, and surrounded by our happiness.

CHAPTER EIGHT

Ryan leaves early, kissing me tenderly on my forehead before he goes, leaving me in the warmth of the bed. A couple of hours later, I wake up with a wonderful ache between my thighs. I feel revitalised and refreshed, not bothering to stifle the giggle that escapes my lips as I relive the previous night.

"You finally had your wicked way with Ryan then?" I hear Lexi drawl from the doorway, startling me out of my memories.

I look up to see a feline smirk on her beautiful face, and I return the smile even though my cheeks are flushing.

"Come on, you hussy. Get out of bed, and make yourself presentable. You've an appointment in an hour," she tells me, casually sauntering off.

It takes a second to register what she's said, and when it does, I leap out of bed, throw a robe on, and head to the bathroom.

Half an hour later, I emerge from my room, clean and dressed in loose navy blue corduroy trousers and a cream blouse with a navy silk scarf, courtesy of Justin, and black ankle boots to complete the look.

"What's my appointment?" I ask her as she passes me a croissant in a paper bag with Maxine's on the front. I've no idea why but it's only just occurred to me to ask. I probably should take charge of my life a bit more.

"Your midwife appointment, silly!" she mockingly scolds me.

"Oh." That's when I remember what Grey had said about calling someone he knew in the morning.

We head out of the apartment building into a brisk autumn wind that whips both of our hair around us. Luckily, there's a car waiting for us at the curb, so we quickly hop into it and out of the cold. I see the driver is Sean again, and after a brief hello, we drive off.

About thirty minutes later, Sean pulls up outside a tall brick mid-terrace building with a shiny red front door. As we get out and walk up the few steps, I see a brass plaque that reads 'Dr. Phillip Evans MD'. The door opens as we approach, and in the doorway stands a woman in her mid-forties, her blonde hair in a neat bun, and wearing rose pink scrubs.

"Welcome," she greets us, smiling warmly. "You must be Laura Darling?" she questions me politely, and I nod in response. "Excellent. Follow me please, Doctor Evans is ready for you."

She leads the way into the building, past a small reception area, and down a bright corridor. Pausing in front of a white painted door, she knocks once then enters.

"Laura's here, Doctor," she says cheerfully.

I notice an older distinguished looking gentleman sitting behind a wooden desk. He's wearing a light blue shirt with a navy blue patterned tie and a white lab coat. Dr. Evans looks up as Lexi and I walk in, a broad reassuring smile on his face, he gets up and holds out his hand for me to shake.

"Laura, a pleasure, and congratulations," he beams at me in cultured tones. "I'm Dr. Evans, and I'll be your consultant for the duration of your pregnancy. Although, you'll mostly see Sally here, your midwife, unless any complications come up. Which, given your age, I highly doubt. Now, take a seat. You can tell me what you know, and we shall take it from there."

The next twenty minutes or so is taken up with form filling and relaying my medical history. The nurse takes some blood and a urine sample, then it's time to hop up on the bed and have the examination part of the consultation. Nervous butterflies flutter around in my stomach as I pull my trousers to below my hips.

Once I'm settled, Dr. Evans takes out some kind of monitor, squirting some cold jelly onto my lower stomach.

"Let's have a look, shall we?" he says as he puts the wand onto the jelly and starts moving it around.

Within moments, I hear the fast sonic sounding beat of my baby's heart, and tears rush to my eyes. For the first time, this feels real; there's actually a life growing inside of me.

"Lexi," I quietly whisper and glanced up to see her right beside me, her own eyes misted with happy tears.

"Oh love, that's your baby," she murmurs back, voice thick as she grasps my hand and squeezes.

I lay there, letting the rhythm surround me like a magical blanket, soothing my soul. All too soon the doctor pulls the wand away, passing me some tissue to wipe the gel off.

"Heartbeat is strong and good, so all is well," he declares, and I feel a rush of relief flood through me. I didn't even realise that I was worried, but I feel elated to discover that everything is okay and that my baby is safe and growing.

"That's it, so if you want to get dressed then Sally here will sort out your next appointment," he informs me kindly, turning and heading out of the room.

I feel as though I'm on cloud nine the whole journey back home, and even Lexi can't stop smiling.

"Have you thought more about Grey's offer, hun?" she gently asks as we walk into the apartment.

"I think," I say, biting my lower lip in apprehension, "I'd like to give it a go." She squeals, grabbing my hands and spinning me around, then apologising and saying something about being careful of the baby.

"Although, I'm not sure about taking my clothes off," I tell her, an idea that came to me this morning bubbling up to the surface of my mind as I speak. "But when I was in boarding school, we had a drama teacher, Mrs. Sin, who taught us belly dancing."

"Belly dancing?" she quirks a brow at me in confusion. "But, hun, Grey's is, well, a strip club."

"I know, but this kind of dancing is pretty sensual, and I've seen YouTube videos of pregnant women doing it and they're pretty hot," I justify, and I can see the cogs starting to turn in her mind as a twinkle enters her eye.

"Oh! Justin can dress you as a kind of fertility goddess! Dark makeup, green silk, and headdresses!" she enthuses, getting more excited as she speaks.

"Sure," I chuckle back, also warming to the idea now that I've spoken it aloud.

I feel a flutter in my stomach, and it takes me a moment to realise it's not the usual butterflies but my baby. My hand flies to cover my stomach, trying to feel anything on the outside, but it's not quite strong enough yet.

"Looks like the baby approves!" Lexi laughs.

Looks like baby does, I think with a smile, my hand stroking my slightly rounded stomach.

CHAPTER NINE

A week later, I'm regretting my decision whilst Justin puts the finishing touches on my fertility goddess outfit. As Lexi suggested, I'm wearing a moss green silk skirt that is basically a collection of scarves attached to a waistband of gold that sits on my hips underneath my stomach and accentuating the slight roundness. There's a matching bra, with sheer tendrils of fabric that hang down and tickle my torso. My makeup is dark, and my freshly dyed red hair is up in an elaborate updo with a sort of gold crown in the shape of twigs and leaves nestled into it. Hanging from the crown is another sheer scarf that covers my face from under my eyes, down to my chin. That addition was mine, just on the off chance anyone from my past comes in.

"You look like a fucking goddess!" Lexi squeals, taking me in as I stand in front of the mirror whilst Justin fixes the small anklet of bells around my ankle. I'm barefoot, which is a relief as I doubt I'd be able to wear the high heeled shoes the others do.

"T-thanks," I manage to stammer out, feeling a little queasy. I do feel pretty attractive, and there is something sexy about the hint my slightly rounded stomach gives.

"Showtime," I hear Grey say from the doorway, and I catch his gaze in the mirror. "You look beautiful, Laura," he tells me with a kind and appreciative smile.

"Thank you, Grey," I whisper back, taking a steadying breath and turning around to walk out the door.

I head towards the back staircase, which is for staff use only, leading down into the basement. The whole room is soundproof, so it's not until the door at the bottom is opened that I can hear all the chatter. The others go ahead of me, taking up positions on their various tables around the room. We decided that we'd all dance to the music suited to belly dancing, but that I would come in as the music starts, dancing my way to my table.

The music begins, and I step through the door, nerves fluttering in my stomach. A hand stops me, and I look up to see Ryan's chocolate brown eyes staring down at me.

"You look fucking gorgeous, Laura," he rasps out, his eyes scorching me as they slide down and then back up my body. "Dance for me tonight," he orders, and I give him a nod then start my routine.

Rolling my hips in time with the music, I dance my way up the steps that lead to the table's surface. I move in a slow circle, taking in the men sitting around me, and see hunger and appreciation in their eyes which widen as I move my hands in such a way as to highlight my rounded stomach.

One, in particular, a dark haired man in a suit, sits up straighter, his nostrils flaring as he takes me in. He's completely ignoring the suited gentleman beside him who is trying to talk to him about something. I don't hold his gaze for long; there's an intensity to it that leaves me feeling unnerved. Like I am a prize to be taken home and locked up.

I look up and seek out Ryan's gaze as I twist and turn, doing a couple of stomach rolls and turning my hands in circles above me in time to the beat. It feels incredible being up here and so openly admired, and I get lost in the dance and the freedom that I'm feeling down to my very soul. It's unlike anything that I have ever experienced before and gives me such a heady rush that I understand why the others enjoy dancing like this.

The song draws to a close, and I end my dance, out of breath but elated. I make my way down the steps to find Mr. Dark and Intense waiting. He bows his head, handing me a wad of banknotes.

"Until next time, Aphrodite," he whispers, his voice deep and dark like wind whispering around gravestones on a moonless night.

I shudder but take the cash, and I swear I can feel his eyes follow me as I head towards Ryan and the stairs.

CHAPTER TEN

The next few weeks continue in the same way, me dancing a couple of times over the course of the night, all while my stomach gets rounder with the baby growing inside of me. I've started to feel more movements, and the first time Lexi felt my baby kick, we both ended up in tears at the sheer magic of it.

I've also had both my scans and seeing my baby on the screen, watching the baby wriggle around and knowing that it's healthy and where it needs to be, created such a wealth of happiness in my chest, I thought that I might burst. I decided not to find out whether it's a boy or girl. We get so few surprises in life, I wanted this to be one of them.

I've entered that glowing phase that everyone talks about, and I really do feel great. My hair is thicker, my boobs are getting bigger and rounder, much to Ryan's appreciation on the nights he's had *coffee*. I generally feel well, and I'm grateful that the need to pee every two seconds has passed. I also no longer seem to have any queasiness at all, not that I had much but it was miserable when I did. It's a strange feeling having your body no longer be your own, although there's a comfort in knowing that no matter what, I am no longer alone in this world.

My now obvious pregnancy seems to draw more members my way. Grey really was right when he said that a lot of men would find it attractive. The table I dance on is always full, with some members requesting a seat specifically. Lexi jokes that she needs to get knocked up and that they've all been missing a trick all these years!

I bring in a huge amount of tips, it's crazy really what the rich will spend their money on, and my best tipper is the brooding mysterious guy from that first night. He's always at my table, watching me with his dark, predatory gaze, his intense eyes fixed on my body the whole time. I asked Lexi about him, and apparently, he's some kind of billionaire who uses the club for business meetings mostly, though no one is quite sure what his business actually is. His name is Mr. Black; each member is given an alias in the form of a different colour, and no one but Grey knows who they really are.

I'm not sure whether or not I should be worried by his unwavering attention. He never steps out of line, only touches me to help me down from the table and to place his wad of cash into my hand. He's not done anything to warrant the feeling of uneasiness that he inspires in me, yet I feel it all the same.

Ryan doesn't like it, although he's trying to keep his possessiveness in check. He's staying with me a lot in my bed, always leaving before I'm up. He says seeing me dance night after night gives him dickache, like a headache but with his dick, so it's my own fault really. *Cheeky bugger!*

I've just finished getting ready for my dance tonight, grateful that I'm in the dry and warm club, with the cold December wind blowing and sleet falling from the sky outside.

"You're up, doll," Justin tells me, then rushes off to help a new girl who's in a muddle with her suspenders.

The baby gives me a little kick as if to tell me to hurry up, and I chuckle to myself at its seeming impatience. I make my way downstairs to the basement, seeing Ryan as usual once I step past the doorway. He trails his fingers across my stomach sending flutters of pleasure skittering across my abdomen and into my core. I see him smirk in a satisfied male way as he hears my breath hitch.

My song comes on, a sensual piece with the rhythmic pounding of drums so I make my way to my table, rolling my hips in time with the beat as I walk. Dancing up the small steps to the table, I take note of Mr. Black who is here as expected. I give him a small nod, which he returns with a tilt of his lips, an almost smile. There are three other men around the table, all in dark suits, one of whom is seated next to Mr. Black, turned to face him as they speak.

My steps falter as he registers where Black's attention has gone and faces me. *Shit! Fuck!* It's Julian Vanderbilt, CEO of Black Knight Corporation and one of Ace's associates. I've met this man on countless occasions, spoken to his wife, and sat down to dinner at their house. His eyes alight with appreciation but not recognition, at least, I don't think they do but my panic is colouring my judgement.

My heart pounds in time with the drums, and I see Ryan heading in my direction, his face wreathed with concern. I look at him and shake my head, taking a deep breath and continuing to dance. My eyes catch Black's, and I can see he's sitting stock still, his own eyes tumultuous and full of what looks like anger which confuses me.

The song comes to an end, and I hurry over to the steps to find Black waiting, as usual, to help me down. My hand shakes as it clasps his, and when I reach the bottom, he leans in close to my ear, keeping hold of my hand.

"Apologies, Aphrodite, he will not come here again," he whispers darkly before handing me the usual wad of bills and releasing his grip.

I don't say anything in return, my mouth unable to utter a word, then I walk off, trying to appear casual whilst my insides churn with worry and fear.

As I go to step past Ryan, he grabs my upper arm, stepping through the door with me and closing it behind us.

"What happened? Are you okay?" he asks, cupping my jaw, worry shining in his brown eyes. "Is the baby okay?"

"Just a misstep, nothing to worry about." I try to assure him by smiling, but my heart still pounds in fear of being discovered. I know my smile falls short when he doesn't look reassured and, if anything, looks more concerned.

"One day, I hope you trust me enough to tell me about your past. You're not alone anymore, Laura, and I can protect you," he tells me vehemently, not giving me a chance to answer before he presses a light kiss on my lips then heads back out the door.

It's not me that needs protecting the most, I think as I stare after him, holding my stomach and feeling the life inside me move.

CHAPTER ELEVEN

Christmas and New Year come and go. Black is true to his word, and I don't see Julian at Grey's again. As the weeks roll by, I start to relax when there are no apparent repercussions, so I can only hope that means that he didn't recognise me.

Lexi and I spend a wonderful Christmas at the apartment, stuffing our faces until we can't move, not that I can move with any speed these days anyway. We don't get dressed all day, slobbing out and watching sappy movies. We exchanged gifts; I got her a sexy little leopard print romper and matching eye mask from Agent Provocateur. I got Ryan, well, myself I suppose, a little lacy teddy for me to wear the next time he's over, also from Agent Provocateur.

We spent New Year's Eve working at Grey's. It's one of the biggest parties of the year for us, and we both make a fortune. I even get a kiss at midnight from Ryan when he pulls me to a dark corner and steals my breath away, devouring my lips and mouth.

I still haven't committed to him, which I feel terrible for. I'm not seeing anyone else, neither is he as far as I can tell, but I just don't feel like it's safe to be together officially. I mean, everyone knows we are sleeping with each other, but that's it. If Ace does find me, which admittedly is looking less likely the more time passes, he would destroy Ryan, hurting him horribly, and I can't risk that. I care for him too much. Plus there are my lingering feelings for Tom…and the guilt whenever I think about him when I'm with Ryan.

Spring is finally here, and I'm officially as big as a whale! I'm actually considering if I should stop dancing, as I feel so cumbersome and like it's time to focus on the impending arrival of my baby. There's less than a month until my due date, and although I know that babies aren't always on time, Grey did say I could take maternity leave, so I think maybe I should.

I feel lighter having made that decision. The next morning, I'm woken early by a strong pain tearing across my stomach, ending with a dull ache in my pelvis. Groaning quietly so as not to wake Ryan who's asleep next to me, I get up and head to the toilet. When I wipe myself, I see the evidence of what the midwife called my plug; basically, slightly bloody goo.

"Lexi!" I shriek, staring down at the tissue. Moments later the door bangs open, Lexi standing there dishevelled, her hair wild, and I hold it out to show her. "Look!"

"Okay, gorgeous," she says, eyes wide and voice shaky. "Let's keep calm and call Sally."

We discussed having a home birth at the apartment with her, which she was very supportive of. Lexi goes off to make the call whilst I clean up, going back into my room to find Ryan sitting on the edge of the bed wide awake.

"Will you stay with me?" I ask him, suddenly needing his strong presence around me as I go through this.

"Of course," he says immediately, getting up and enfolding me in his big arms, holding me tightly. Another pain flashes across my abdomen, but it's manageable. "Want me to run you a bath?" he asks, leaning back to look at me.

"That would be perfect," I whisper gratefully, suddenly a little scared and unsure now that the day has come.

He takes my hand and leads me back into the bathroom, turning on the taps and running me a bath that is the perfect temperature. As I'm getting in, Lexi comes back, telling me that Sally said to give her a call when I'm having roughly three contractions within ten minutes. I nod, then soak in the tub for a while, letting the hot water soothe my body and calm my nerves. Ryan doesn't leave my side, chatting gently to me and successfully keeping my mind occupied.

Getting out, he helps me dry off, wrapping me in my big fluffy dressing gown and cashmere socks that Lexi got me for Christmas. We walk towards the rest of the apartment, and I gasp as I see what Lexi has done, tears filling my eyes. The whole place is darkened with only dim lamps and fairy lights casting a soft glow on the main living space. There are cards with positive messages everywhere and soft classical music is playing. I can see on the kitchen countertop is an array of healthy snacks, some chocolate, and vitamin drinks.

"Lexi..." I choke out, lost for words.

"I hope it's okay?" she gently asks, her tone unsure. "I looked up online about calm home birth spaces, and all these things were suggested," she tells me.

"It's...it's beautiful and perfect. Thank you." I take her hands in mine and squeeze them. She beams back at me, her own eyes glistening. I gasp as another pain hits, causing me to squeeze her hands a little tighter.

"Right," she says after the pain has passed. "Remember, Sally said to keep moving. Do you want to have something to eat then go for a walk and get some fresh air?"

I nod, thinking that sounds exactly like what I need.

We come back from the walk when I have to keep stopping to breathe through the ever increasingly painful contractions. I get changed into loose PJ bottoms and a tank top, continuing to walk around the apartment with Ryan supporting me. The contractions have picked up. I'm not sure how frequent they are, but Lexi decides to call Sally who says she'll be over in about half an hour.

A couple of minutes after that, the pain changes and becomes a lot more urgent. I keep breathing, although it feels harder now as there's very little let up. I feel the immediate need to squat down like something is coming.

"Lexi!" I manage to gasp out, and she rushes towards me looking at me hunched over, gripping Ryan's arms tightly.

"Are you pushing, Laura?" she asks, and I don't know how to answer that as another pain hits because I do feel the urgent need to push down.

Not fully aware of what I'm doing, my body has taken over. I pushed my PJ bottoms down and kicked them off, then got onto my knees in front of the sofa. I vaguely hear someone curse as I scream out, pain tearing my body into two, my opening burning. I move one hand between my legs, and I can feel something round emerging from between my thighs. *I can't be ready! First-borns take longer, that's what everyone said!*

I feel a strong grip on my other hand, and I look up into calming chocolate brown eyes. I don't have time to register more than that. I can hear Lexi on the phone right behind me when another searing pain tears through me. The hand between my legs comes up and I grip Ryan's other one with my own, changing position slightly. With a scream, I feel my baby slide out with a rush of wetness.

"Come here, little one," I hear Lexi coo over my rushing heartbeat and panting breaths.

A second passes, then I hear the wonderful wail of a newborn baby, angry at leaving the warmth of the womb. A part laugh, part cry escapes my lips as I let go of Ryan's hands and Lexi passes a wriggling towel-wrapped bundle between my legs, I'm still on my knees, and into my waiting arms. I look down at a bright pink screaming face, and my eyes fill with tears of joy.

I look up at Ryan to see his eyes wet as well. "Boy or girl?" he rasps out, and I unwrap the towel to see that I have a daughter. A beautiful baby girl. I cuddle her to me, feeling a rush of slickness between my legs as Lexi declares the afterbirth has come away.

A few minutes later, I hear the door buzzer go off, and Ryan gets up to answer it. I'm still kneeling on the floor; luckily, Lexi put down waterproof coverings with towels on top over the carpet.

"What's her name?" I hear Lexi say softly from beside me, and I look up from my baby who has settled down a little now.

"Lilly, her name is Lilly Darling."

CHAPTER TWELVE
18 YEARS LATER...

"Fuck you!" Lilly screams at me, the sound of our front door slamming closed as I stand, leaning my hands on the kitchen counter and trying to calm my anger and terror.

My hands clenched in fists of anger and concern, one shaking around the newspaper clipping I'm clutching tightly. It's an article about an award for a creative writing competition that Lilly won. It's already two weeks old, and she had it hidden in her room. I hate that she felt like she had to hide it, knowing that I would freak out, but it's for the best that there are no images of her anywhere. She's not allowed any social media accounts, which we've fought over, and I can never give her a good enough answer. She looks so much like me, and although it's been almost seventeen years since I ran, Ace's reach is endless.

I've tried to keep us safe, by being anonymous, but of course, Lilly just sees an overbearing and controlling mother who's trying to ruin her life, as most teenagers think when it comes to their parents. How can I tell her that her father is not absent, but a monster that I had to escape from? It's been the hardest thing to keep from her, but it's what keeps her safe and that is my priority.

We've been fighting so much recently, and not just about my refusal to let her get Facebook, or Tik Tok, or whatever it is she wants to post pictures of her life onto. She hates that I won't commit to Ryan fully, I still can't bring myself to put him in that kind of danger. He knows something happened, I've never fully divulged my past, but I'm sure he can make an educated guess from the little that I have told him. We're good friends, with a few benefits when Lilly is away for the night at a friend's, which isn't often as I need to know who she's with to make sure that she's safe.

It's all such a mess!

I stay there for what feels like hours but is probably only thirty minutes or so, just breathing, listening to the radio and trying to calm down, when I hear the front door open again. Turning to face her, an apology springs to my lips.

"Lilly, I'm so sor..." I come to a shuddering halt, my whole body flushing with a white-hot terror that freezes me like the burn of ice running through my veins. My heart pounds, and it feels like the whole world has paused on its axis.

"Hello, Violet," his voice is just as dark as I remember from my nightmares, and although older, he's just as devastatingly beautiful, too. His eyes have not changed, if anything they look deader than they used to, like the small shred of humanity that used to be in there is completely snuffed out and gone.

"Ace," I manage to whisper out, my voice broken. "How did you find me?"

"Now, that's just ill-mannered, Violet, not even asking after my well-being, and I know you were brought up better than that. Although, you were also brought up not to steal, whore yourself out, show your body to others..." he trails off like my litany of sins is just too much for him to remember them all. Or like he no longer cares.

His body is loose, like a hunting tiger, as he stalks over to our small kitchen table and sits down, straightening the cuffs of his dark suit jacket like he's at a business meeting. His dark eyes look back up, locking with mine, another chill sweeping over me at the way he looks at me. Like I'm no longer a person, *I wonder if I ever was to him?*

"H-how are you, Ace?" I ask, voice shaking as I slip back into old habits of shrinking into myself and trying to appear small.

He nods his approval. "Well, considering you stole my share in Black Knight Corporation sixteen years ago, not to mention hiding my heir from me, I am not too happy with you, Violet." His eyes cut to me, slicing into me like a honed blade. "It's a shame she's a girl when the others all have male heirs, but some things can't be helped," he adds, almost to himself.

"What?" A fresh wave of terror washes over me. *He knows! How does he know?!*

"Don't be coy, Violet. You left the evidence behind, and you never leave evidence behind," he tells me, anger flashes in his eyes at my refusal to acknowledge Lilly out loud to him.

"I-I don't know what you're talking about," I stammer, flinching when he slams his hands down on the tabletop, his calm disintegrating.

"Don't lie to me, Violet!" he hisses out, suddenly standing up, and I flinch again from the vitriol in his voice and the wild look in his eyes. "You left the test behind, and I found it that night. You never were the smartest woman," he sneers, his hands sliding down the front of his jacket, smoothing out any wrinkles as he sits down again.

Oh god, the test. I'd completely forgotten that I'd hidden it in the cleaning cupboard. And of course, he found it, he always was methodical and thorough.

"I see you've finally remembered," he smirks at me, straightening his tie. "Now, the important thing is you will tell me where the bonds that you stole from me are, and we can maybe put all this unpleasantness behind us." I swallow as his eyes flit back up, boring into me like he can dig the information out of my brain.

"No," I reply, my eyes flitting around to try and find my phone. If I could only call Lexi or Ryan, I may be able to get help. Thank god Lilly is out with friends, even if I don't know where exactly.

"No?" he questions, tone sharp and a tic twitching next to his right eye.

"I-I won't give them to you. They're Lilly's," I say more firmly, standing up a little straighter. He bullied me for years, and I don't have to take it anymore. I have a life now with people who care about me, and those bonds are mine by right. My money was used to purchase them after all. And they're Lilly's future.

"They are not Lilly's," he spits, standing up once again and taking menacing steps towards me. "They are mine, and you stole them from me. Enough with this little game, Violet. You'll give them back to me, now!"

I hear *Every Breath You Take* by Chase Holfelder come on the radio in the silence as he reaches me, standing so close I can see the slight stubble on his cheek.

"No," I say again, knowing that if I give in, he will have won and running would have been all for nothing. They are Lilly's security, something to ensure her comfort in life. "I'll never give them to you, and you'll never find them."

"It's my fucking business!" he screams, and he's so close that I feel spittle land on my cheek. "You stole it from me, you worthless bitch. I earned it, I fucking earned it! I took the risks! I took the paths no one else dared to!" His eyes are wild, his veins bulging in his neck. "Do you want to know why I'm so successful? I am like a fucking surgeon, Violet; clinical, detached, precise. I take what doesn't work and cut it away, dispose of it. How dare you question me? Steal from me? Take what is mine?" he's panting, and I watch as he seems to calm himself down, taking in a great lungful of air.

He laughs then, and it's a cruel sound full of shards of broken glass and poison. It makes me wince. It's so cutting. His cheeks are flushed, and his hands clench and unclench into fists.

He leans in so that his lips are next to my ear. "Oh, I'll find the bonds, Violet, just like I was able to find you," he whispers in a lover's caress that leaves me queasy and shaking. He leans back, his eyes looking away from me.

"You'll never get your hands on them, Ace, I can guarantee you that," my voice is firm, and I realise that I'm not scared of him. Not anymore.

I see the glint of silver in the corner of my eye seconds before a line of fire races across my chest. Gasping, my hand flies to the pain only to come away stained with red. I look up at Ace to see the silver of one of my kitchen knives in his hand, dripping with blood. My blood. I watch with frightened eyes as it comes down towards me, as if in slow motion, unable to stop it as it enters my stomach smoothly. I grunt with the impact, but there's no fire this time, just a sort of fascination as he pulls it back out, blood pouring out of me and splattering the floor.

My knees give way, and I land on them on the lino tiles that I'd only cleaned that morning. Vaguely, I hear the haunting tones of Akine singing *Devil Like Me*. *I love this song*, I think as I sink down onto my side, then roll onto my back. The sunlight coming in from the window waves and undulates as it's filtered through the trees outside, creating beautiful patterns across the ceiling.

Vaguely, I register another impact on my body, then another and another, but there's no more pain. I think there should be, and for a brief moment, my body panics but the comforting numbness soon returns.

Oh Lilly, I think with sorrow. *My beautiful Lilly flower. I'm so sorry for leaving you.* I know a moment of true regret with the realisation that I'm leaving her all alone. *Not completely alone*, I remember as my mind supplies Lexi and Ryan's faces flashing before me. I feel my lips pull into a smile before they disappear to be replaced with the face of the devil.

"I'll be sure to keep a close eye on our daughter," he says, voice soft, and I think that I should feel terror at that statement. But all I feel is the darkness coming to wrap me in its comforting embrace.

. . .

Want to know what happens to Lilly next? Read Captured, Highgate Preparatory Academy, Book 1.

And to keep up to date with all my news, sign up for my newsletter at www.rosaleeauthor.com/newsletter-sign-up

AUTHOR NOTE

How are we feeling after that? I know, I know, you may hate me a little bit (especially if you went in blind and haven't red the rest of the series yet.)

I'd say that I'm sorry, but Laura's/Violet's story needed to be told, and sometimes it hurts...

ABOUT THE AUTHOR

About Rosa

Rosa Lee lives in a sleepy Wiltshire village, surrounded by the beautiful English countryside and the sound of British Army tanks firing in the background (it's worth the noise for the uniformed dads in the local supermarket and doing the school run!).

Rosa loves writing dark and delicious whychoose romance, and has so many ideas trying to burst out that she can often be found making a note of them as soon as one of her three womb monsters wakes her up. She believes in silver linings and fairytale endings…you know, where the villains claim the Princess for their own, tying her up and destroying the world for her.

If you'd like to know more, please check out Rosa's socials or visit
www.rosaleeauthor.com
Rosa's Captivating Roses
Linktree

ALSO BY ROSA LEE

Also by Rosa

HIGHGATE PREPARATORY ACADEMY

A dark whychoose romance

Hunted: A Highgate Preparatory Academy Prequel

Captured: Highgate Preparatory Academy, Book 1

Bound: Highgate Preparatory Academy, Book 2

Released: Highgate Preparatory Academy, Book 3

DEAD SOLDIERS VS TAILORS DUET

A dark whychoose enemies to lovers romance

Addicted to the Pain

Addicted to the Ruin

THE SHADOWMEN

A dark gang & mafia whychoose romance

Kissed by Shadows

Claimed by Shadows

Owned by Shadows

STANDALONES

A dark whychoose Lady and the Tramp(s) retelling

Tainted Saints

A dark whychoose stepbrother Cinderella retelling

Tarnished Embers

A dark whychoose mafia romance Co-written with Mallory Fox

A Night of Revelry and Envy

Printed in Great Britain
by Amazon